The Prince Frog

Written by Ali Sparkes

Illustrated by Jordan Kincaid

Collins

Chapter 1

Many had hoped to marry Princess Freida. She was considered the most intelligent and beautiful young woman in the land. She was a great dancer, too.

She was an awful kisser, though. If you were a frog.

Imagine a big, wet, sloppy mouth, bigger than your head, coming straight at you. Francis would never have rescued her golden ball from the pond if he'd known she was a princess.

Old frogs in the pond had heard warnings about princesses. Apparently, princesses had a thing for kissing frogs just in case they magically turned into handsome princes.

Francis hadn't believed it – until Princess Freida *actually kissed him*. And moments later, he HAD turned into a handsome prince.

It was the worst day of his life.

Chapter 2

"Oh, darling, *do* try again!"
Princess Freida squeezed his shoulder.
"Come on … I, Prince Francis, do take
thee …"

"I, Prince Frrr … Prince FrrRRRRIBBET!
RIBBET-RIBBET!" said Prince Francis.

Princess Freida buried her face in
her hands. She'd been trying to teach
him their vows for weeks – but basic
human words were hard enough, let
alone all the fancy words he needed
for the wedding.

Sometimes she wasn't completely
sure she even wanted all this
wedding business.

"Tamzara never said it would be
like this!" sighed Princess Freida.
"It was meant to be happy ever after!
She said my prince would be
transformed from a frog. She didn't
say he would still *sound* like a frog."

She ran to the arched window and stared across the palace gardens which were filled with pretty blossoming trees, elegant statues and a large pond with a fountain at the centre ... which Prince Francis had once called home.

He followed her and patted her on the back. He hated to upset her.

"I'm sorry, Francis," she said. "I know you can't help it. You are SO handsome, maybe the other princesses won't *notice* that you're still a bit ... froggy.
Oh ... why is it all so hard?" She sank onto the windowsill. "Everyone expects princesses to be perfect. And now I've made you a prince they'll expect *you* to be perfect, too ..." She lifted her chin. "But you *will* be perfect! I know you will." She smiled up at him.

Prince Francis smiled back and then licked a fat bluebottle off the window and ate it.

Chapter 3

Freida's three big sisters had done as they were told and married the most handsome princes in the land. Now only a few boring dukes were left over – all quite dull and bossy. She couldn't bear to marry any of them. In fact, she secretly wished not to marry at all … she would much rather have become a marine biologist. But the queen insisted. So Freida went to her fairy godmother, Tamzara.

Tamzara cast a spell. Freida was told to catch a frog and kiss it. The spell had worked. Kind of …

"Francis," said Princess Freida, as they walked in the gardens. "Are you … happy? Do you *want* to live happily ever after with me?"

Prince Francis struggled to answer. He was very fond of his fiancée, but inside he was still a frog. He missed the green pondweed tickling his face. He missed shooting around in the silky cool water, snapping up flies from the surface. He missed his frog family.

But every time he tried to go home, a gardener waded in and "saved" him.

Princess Freida caught him staring at the pond again. "Francis ... please don't," she said.

"I do hope," said a cold voice, "you're not thinking about going swimming again, Prince Francis."

The queen was staring at them both, narrowing her eyes.

"He's not!" said Princess Freida, grabbing his hand.

The queen snorted. Then she declared: "I am going to have the pond drained. There will be no ponds. No lakes. No streams or rivers. Not even a well. Once all the water is gone, you'll forget your old life and be happy with my daughter."

"No!" croaked Prince Francis, horrified. "Nooooo!" Then he leapt away.

Chapter 4

As he hopped towards the pond, Francis saw a gardener racing to stop him, so he turned and made for the woods. He leapt into a tree and hid among the leaves.

What could he do? The queen would destroy his old home and everyone in it!

"I didn't know you were a *tree* frog," said a voice.

There was a puff of violet smoke and a sparkly woman appeared on the branch beside him, wearing a purple cloak and carrying a silver wand.

"I'm Tamzara," she said. "Freida's fairy godmother. I turned you into a handsome prince."

Prince Francis sniffed.

"Oh dear," she said. "Don't you *like* being a handsome prince?"

He shook his head. "The queen … wants to … ribbet.
Ribbet." He took a deep breath. "Drain the pond."

The fairy godmother looked concerned. "Well, *that's*
not good. I've got a nice supply of frogs in that pond.
And newts. I need those for my potions."

Prince Francis gave her a hard stare.

"Sorry," she said, clearly remembering he'd recently
been a frog.

"Hey! Move over, you two."

Princess Freida climbed up onto the branch. "I'm so sorry about Mother," she said. "But she *always* gets what she wants. She's going to drain every pond, river and stream. She says I MUST marry a handsome prince and live happily ever after and I … I don't think I'm strong enough to stop her."

Prince Francis struggled to speak. Tamzara tapped him with her wand. Suddenly his words flowed easily.

"Tell her," he gulped, "that I'll never go back to the pond again. I promise. As long as she leaves it alone."

Princess Freida stared at him. "You would promise that?" she said. "You'd never set foot in a pond again … just to save some frogs and newts?"

"Those frogs are my family," said the prince. "And the newts were my friends."

Tamzara suddenly said: "Do you *really* want to spend your life with this man, Freida?"

"I do," said Princess Freida. "He's the best prince anyone ever made."

"Hmmm," said Tamzara. "So you definitely want to marry him?"

"Well, I don't actually care about the wedding,"
said Princess Freida. 'But I do love being with him.'
She squeezed Prince Francis's hand and he
squeezed back.

And then they heard the burbling of a big engine.

Chapter 5

A terrible scene was unfolding in the gardens.
By the pond stood a rumbling yellow truck. Two men
in hard hats were poking a long pipe into the water.
It was making a loud slurping noise. The other end
of the pipe was gushing pond water into a massive
glass tank.

"NOOOOO!" screamed Prince Francis, watching fish,
newts and water snails tumbling around the tank
amid the churning water.

Princess Freida and the queen arrived at his side.

"Mother! Stop it!" yelled the princess.

"Darling, it's FINE!" the queen said. "We'll take all the nasty squishy pond life away. He'll forget it was ever there and you'll both be *much* happier."

Princess Freida turned to the queen, taking a deep breath. "Stop this, Mother! Or I will break off the engagement right now!"

The queen looked very surprised. Her daughter had never stood up to her before. She told the men to stop.

"How can you be happy with a husband who wants to live underwater?" she demanded. "This is the only way! He'll forget about this nonsense soon enough."

"No, Mother," said Princess Freida. "I won't let you do it."

Tamzara appeared nearby.

"Tamzara, can you help us?" asked Princess Freida.

"I may have *another* spell," said Tamzara. "But it will only work if you *both* want it to."

"Oh, for goodness sake – do your magic and let's get past all this!" snapped the queen.

"Fine," said the fairy godmother. "This spell will make them both want exactly the same thing."

"Hurrah for that!" called the queen, rolling her eyes.

"Do you both agree to this?" asked Tamzara.

They nodded, holding hands.

"Oh, do get on with it," snapped the queen.

"And *you* promise to leave the pond in peace?" asked Tamzara.

"You have the queen's word," said the queen, with a dismissive wave.

"Prepare yourselves," said Tamzara, wafting her wand.

Everything swirled – purple and sparkling.

When the swirling ended, Princess Freida had never looked happier.

She was a beautiful frog.

Prince Francis was a very handsome frog, too, once again.

As they swam, waterweed stroking their faces, Princess Freida said: "Well ... *now* I understand why you wanted to come back. This is wonderful!"

"Can you be happy here, my princess?" said her Prince Frog. "There'll be no dresses or balls or sisters married to handsome princes."

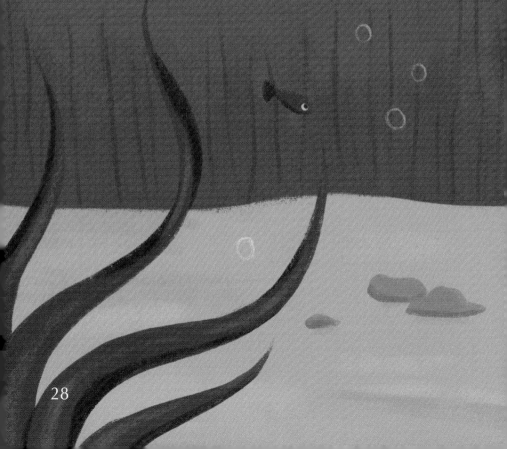

"Do you know what?" Freida said, kicking her long and strong green legs and shooting through bubbles. "I don't think I ever really liked them to begin with."

"Are you sure?" asked her prince.

In reply, Princess Freida snapped up a water beetle.

And they both lived happily ever after.

Freida and Francis

Princess Freida	Prince Francis
desperate to find a prince to please her mum	just wants to be happy in the pond

finds her prince but he's a bit froggy still	just wants to go back to the pond

Princess Freida	Prince Francis
starts to really like Francis for who he is; starts to see she doesn't need to do what her mum wants	starts to really like Freida for who she is

Freida decides to stand up to her mum

Ideas for reading

Written by Gill Matthews
Primary Literacy Consultant

Reading objectives:
- draw on what they already know or on background information and vocabulary provided by the teacher
- make inferences on the basis of what is being said and done
- participate in discussion about books, poems and other works that are read to them and those that they can read for themselves, taking turns and listening to what others say

Spoken language objectives:
- articulate and justify answers, arguments and opinions
- use spoken language to develop understanding through speculating, hypothesising, imagining and exploring ideas
- participate in discussions, presentations, performances, role play, improvisations and debates

Curriculum links: Science: Living things and their habitats

Interest words: screamed, yelled, demanded, snapped

Build a context for reading

- Ask children to look at the front cover of the book and to read the title. Discuss whether it reminds them of any other stories they have read. If children are familiar with the traditional tale *The Frog Prince*, talk about what happens in the story.
- Read the back-cover blurb. Ask children what they think might happen in the story in light of the blurb.
- Point out that this is a modern fairy tale. Explore what children know about traditional fairy tales: typical characters, themes and events. Ask how they think a modern fairy tale might be different from a traditional version.

Understand and apply reading strategies

- Read pp2–5 aloud. Explore children's understanding of what has happened. Ask why they think that the day Princess Freida kissed Francis was the worst day of his life.